Spring Again

Spring Again

발행일	2017년 9월 6일
지은이	변 자 윤
펴낸이	손 형 국
펴낸곳	(주)북랩
편집인	선일영 편집 이종무, 권혁신, 송재병, 최예은, 이소현
디자인	이현수, 김민하, 이정아, 한수희 제작 박기성, 황동현, 구성우
마케팅	김회란, 박진관, 김한결
출판등록	2004. 12. 1(제2012-000051호)
주소	서울시 금천구 가산디지털 1로 168, 우림라이온스밸리 B동 B113, 114호
홈페이지	www.book.co.kr
전화번호	(02)2026-5777 팩스 (02)2026-5747

ISBN   979-11-5987-778-0 03810 (종이책)   979-11-5987-779-7 05810 (전자책)

Spring Again

Jayoon Byeon

북랩 book Lab

 *Spring*

1. [NOUN] the season between winter and summer when the weather becomes warmer, plants start to grow again, and Jayoon starts to write again.

2. [VERB] to jump upward or forward suddenly or quickly.

Foreword

I am very excited to introduce you to Jayoon Byeon's latest book of poetry. I have known Jayoon since she was a college freshman, and she has been a student in many of my classes since. She is a sensitive reader of literature, and she writes from her heart. In this latest collection, Jayoon's poems burst from the pages, fresh, excited, and exciting. Her poems are contagious: when she writes about spring or love, I feel that I am there with her, in the first shy emergence of buds, or the surprising confusions of emotion. Her poems are active, alive, and energetic, brimming with all of life's adventures. I welcome you to join me on the wonderful journey of entering Jayoon's world.

Hyungji Park
Professor of English Literature
Yonsei University

Sitting in my office reading Jayoon's first book, *The Attic Inside*, I was 16 again. In her innocent voice, she shares the growing pains and pleasures of love and friendship. Her second book, *Spring Again*, is written with more confidence and maturity. Each poem tells a story about her life and experiences as she embarks on a new adventure after high school. Each word is carefully chosen to express her feelings and emotions from discovering her passions to falling in love. Jayoon's poems are creative and beautifully written. Through her personal stories, Jayoon is able to connect with readers of all ages – her vivid imagery and lyrical intensity reminds us of love, regret, and hope.

Tae H. Lee
Assistant Professor
Dept. of English Language & Literature
Yonsei University

Preface

Four springs have passed since my last book, *The Attic Inside*, was born. A lot has changed since then. I graduated from high school and entered university. I was able to see parts of the world I had never seen before. I encountered various feelings that were new and unexpected, and I am slowly learning about how to handle these emotions with care, at my own pace. Each spring has gifted me with unforgettable memories and lessons.

The first part of *Spring Again*, Innocence, is consisted of stories from my late teenage and college freshman years. The second part, Blossom, features pieces mostly written in the last two years. While *The Attic Inside* mostly speaks about love from a teenage girl's perspective, I have tried to experiment with relatively diverse topics, forms, and atmospheres in *Spring Again*.

I sincerely hope that the readers enjoy traveling through my written moments as much as I enjoyed recreating them on paper.

With love,
Jayoon

Contents

Part 2. **Blossom**

Part 1

Innocence

—

And since you walked into my life last May
you have been the only one that stayed.

Greetings from Seoul to New York

How are you, I shall say
I have not seen you for a while.
I chose to say hello this way
I hope you are doing just fine.

A city of Broadway, Times Square,
and the Statue of Liberty—
Don't you find the atmosphere quite rare?
You will explore a new self, hopefully.

From a so-called city that never sleeps
You will return with a dream-filled soul.
For you, I have put together this greeting
A letter sent all the way from Seoul.

Miles to Go Before She Sleeps

Listen to this story of a thirtysome woman.
She's got a job, but it's no career.
She constantly tells herself, "Come on—
Why waste all these years?"

She must keep his poem in mind—
He'd said, 'I have miles to go before I sleep.'
Applies to her the same, she deserves more—
So why is she only standing still?

This poem was inspired by Robert Frost's poem, 'Stopping by Woods on a Snowy Evening.'

Lodestar

You, the blood in my veins
teach me to invincible
guiding me through the dark and the pains.

You have grown me strong
during all this time we have shared—
neither too short nor too long.

Yes, I used to be insecure, but
you give me strength, you raise me up
to stand up tall, to try once more.

You could probably tell
from the look in my eye, but
how blessed I am
to have you in my life.

18

Spring Again

An Eagle's Wingbeat

The vortex nears.

He's pushed toward the edge, forced to leave
as the wind thrashes him with its merciless hands.
He pants, runs out of air to breathe—
He's left with scars no time can mend.

His biggest fear has been being let-down;
He's always been an avoider of high hopes.
But for once, he stretches a claw out toward the crown
and soars up as high as he can go.

He may crash, break, drop straight down—
shattered to the point he cannot move.
But for once, he pushes away the voices in doubt,
ready for any salt on his wounds.

You Stayed

Bad news comes fast with a click.
Staring into the monitor, all I can do is blink.
Surprisingly enough, tears do not come
as if what I'm seeing is only an illusion.

I tell them I'm alright, smile and all
but with shaking hands make a call.
Though you pick up with a tone injured
soon I realize, you're the only one concerned.

Misgivings are all I can talk about
as you try your best to calm me down.
And I receive your message on the phone
when I'm dejectedly walking all the way home.

It reads: All will be well, just wait and see,
you may as well stay calm and stop crying.
Just when I think I've cried enough
I begin all over again, holding onto your words.

Two months later, you proved yourself right
and painted my sky blue with a knowing smile.

And since you walked into my life last May
you have been the only one that stayed.

Graduation

Throughout the most troublous time of my life
You have been a shoulder to cry on;
You taught me the warmth of someone.

No promises were ever made—
Still, you proved that I could trust you,
rest my weathered soul upon you.

The pitiless calendar runs out of pages to turn
and I stand before an end of a long road.
I drop on my knees, unable to carry on.

But as you stand behind, cheer and wave
I wipe my tears, hide my fears, and smile—

The time has come
to kiss you goodbye.

Ode to a Young Poet

Don't you see it beginning?

Yellow hair, tousled
Crescent eyes, full of mischief
The day I met you.

Midnight falls, we're awake
You insist, I stare across
I'm no Miss Right for you.

Eyes meet, blushing
Heart beats, you only laugh
Let's talk literature.

Loud music, glasses clink
Right across the table, you
We sing our lungs out.

Oh darling,
Don't you see it beginning?

You are poetry to me.

RAM

The night falls.

In a loose dark-olive tee, I'm sitting down at the back of the room when he comes over and does the same. I'm a little stunned. Is this for real? During the past few years I've know him, never has he come near me with other people around. I've always suspected that he doesn't want to know we're a bit closer than they think we are.

His eyes – normally wide and translucent – are opaque today for an unknown reason. I wonder why for a moment, but shortly put aside the thought as I decide that I like his softer gaze better. As his lips part and my name is called, everyone around us suddenly disappears. He asks me how my project has been going. I tell him about my past achievements and whatnots, hoping he doesn't hear the beat, beat, beat.

I'm trying to participate a lot more this year, I add with a shaking voice. Are you? He asks, softly laughing and stroking my hair. My face reddens at his gaze, affectionate yet intense. I cannot bear to look up, so I give a shrug instead.

cont.

After a moment, he begins to talk about his worries and doubts. I have never seen him look so disturbed. All I do is listen and nod now and then, there being nothing I can do to solve his problems. At the same time, I'm surprised to know he relies on me this much; it's pretty obvious that the words he's speaking to me are coming from his attic inside.

Then, at the same time, I wonder, doesn't he have *her* to talk about these things? An unwelcome visage brushes past my left hemisphere.

You know, his voice rings in the balmiest decibel. I've had a lot of people come talk to me, but I've never met one whom I can relate to as much as you. Really? Though I can hardly contain my joy, I try my best to calm myself down and plaster an easy curve on my lips. A thousand thoughts marathon through my head as he looks me in the eye once again and caressingly brushes my hair back with the most delicate fingers.

That's when I realize that these moments are never to happen in reality. I stifle a lethargic laugh. This man, I think to myself, is too good to be mine, isn't he?

The alarm rings.

The Day I Turned Nineteen

Burgundy dress, cake pops, white wine—
You might think I'm having a great time.
Roses, champagne, silverware—
Do these even matter, when he is not here?

I should be grateful, I know;
Surrounded by people who couldn't love me more.
But look, all I wanted was a small congratulation—
Was I asking for too much?

Then, all of a sudden, the phone rings by my side.
It reads: a new message has arrived.
I squint. I cannot believe my eyes
as my lips spread into a wide smile.

Oh, how few words can make your day!
Three words from him have completed my birthday.

Question, Lingered

Shifting eyes, awkward laughs and smiles;
All this time I was sending signs.
I trace back to the times over and over again;
Weren't you the one who showed interest then?

I call him up but you're the one that comes—
to pick me up and embrace me in your arms.
I asked you to meet me on a Friday night
and you came— wasn't that another sign?

You say you weren't aware of my feelings,
but I'm tired of coming up with hints.
What, do you expect me to get down on my knees
and beg you to love me? Would it make you pleased?

Was I only wrong? Did I get lost in translation
and mistake your honest indifference
for shyness? As I hold onto the silent phone,
one question echoes in my head, leaving me lone.

What am I to you?

Her Tale

'Meet me at the theater on Friday night.
I'll wait, it doesn't matter if you come late.'
You never returned an answer.

Friday night, lobby of the theater,
I wait and wait, my eyes set on the rotating door
hoping it'd be you each time the door opens.
Eventually I lose track of time
and a staff tells me to leave.
I walk out, shoulders slumped and heart weathered,
but my intuition draws me in again.
The glass door opens, I walk in,
the candle-lit hallway leads me into the theater.

Though I cannot see you, I can hear your voice.
What is a film of your choice, you ask
but my lips cannot do much but stutter.
A gentleman's heels
make sounds against the wooden floor
and my heart stops at your presence.
I breathe in, then out,
and tell myself not to look your way.

The lights are off, the film begins.

A Boy's Tale from Boulevard 38

It was a midday of April shower
when the blue tune of your violin
awakened the hollow, darkened mansion.

People, blind and deaf, could never see you
but I could hear your melody loud and clear.

Day and night, I held onto your hand
whispering tales and daydreams in your ears;
words they never cared to understand.

But one night they dragged me away from you
and burned down our tree house.

The name you had come up with;
it was for me, only me.
And the screaming syllables
echo inside my head until

A Mother's Tale from Boulevard 38

It was a midday of April shower
when the dead silence of our mansion was broken;
Our boy spoke for the first time in years.

'I hear a violin,' he repeated and repeated
but no one was to be found in the guest room.

Soon after, he was often found in the garret
murmuring incomprehensible words
his visage white, pupils hollow, hands frigid.

We decided that his illness was coming back
and locked the garret away from him.

Few days later came a cough, a fever,
a goodbye kiss, and we sealed him away.
Rest in peace, little boy. You were a loved child.

Daaé

Christine, Christine—
Bravissima! with a glass of champagne.
The Populaire was filled with magic
as your birdly voice took wings.

Christine, Christine—
Would it be a sin
to bear you in my heart,
to long for you to be mine?

Christine, Christine—
For the absence of your music
will prison my soul in pain,
turn my life to beige.

O.G.

Lunar Eclipse

Whispers from the streets, I heard
and I'm dusting off the drawers inside my head.
It was around this time of the year
when perfect things started to crack, then break.

You pushed me away— Why,
when I believed in you to take me out of the cage?
To find the right path, I tried
but you were another trouble to drive me to the edge.

I was only a child uncertain, stuck inside a maze,
so why did you have to push me away?
The time has run out, take a look at the hourglass;
Your spoken regret has lost its place to stay.

Ode to a Hopeless Hoper

How I wish I could go back in time
and clasp that lousy mouth of mine.
Mood swing? Alcohol? You name the cause;
whichever one led to nothing but chaos.

But can you honestly say all blame is mine?
Really, cross your heart and hope to die?
You were playing against the rules—
I should have known, wasn't I a fool.

You probably bought this book
expecting for yourself a love poem or two.
But you are not worth writing sweet verses for—
that is one fact never to be changed for sure.

ROT

I have become a pretender.
I have learned to sit still,
plaster a fake smile,
pretend to listen.

How dainty of her—
busy chirping about
how big her house is,
how wealthy her parents are.

How does a few Instagram pictures
and numbers printed on a bank account
give you so much dignity?

20, I sit back and only smile.
Suit yourself till the last page;
Let's see who wins the final race.

Again in December

I meet you on a snowy Thursday night,
in a restaurant filled with Christmas lights.
We begin with an awkward hello
both wondering how far this would go.

For two hours and a half,
I am no one else but myself
as we talk Les Misérables, friends in common,
Lena Park, Yeats, phoneme, and so on.

Giggles and small talks as you walk me home
with a pace just right, neither fast nor slow.
I know it's too early to conclude anything,
but am I the only one to sense a beginning?

Too many scars still here to mend,
My middle name has been Break and End.
But you make me want to believe again
and I hope, for you, it's the same.

2015

Trapped inside a dark room
I could hardly breathe;
I screamed and cried,
I could do nothing but grieve.

Then you knocked on my door
with all you could offer.
You stood tall and firm
for someone who forgot how to believe.

But again, the wet blackness took over
and I had to make you leave.
The fault is no one's but mine;
all had gone too far to redeem.

So here I am,
as usual, left, all by myself
with nothing but
memories to relive.

Single Ring

A quarter has passed.

I am walking home
bracing a deserted soul
when I see your face in the crowd.

In a brief second as I walk past
all surrounding people are enclosed
and it's you, only you that I see.

And the times I spent writing poems about you
race back to my mind.

I turn around
cross the street
walk back to you
and call your name out.

Salutations and a bright smile,
both surprisingly genuine.

The traffic light turns green again
and we turn around from each other
to go on separate ways.

I bid you the good in goodbye;
That's when I could finally set myself free.

I never looked back.

Part 2

Blossom

I wish I did not have to travel to
the artistic city you live in.

Spring Elegy I

Wednesday afternoon you caught my eye
then memorized my scent.
The next day, I memorized yours.
A week later, you fell for me.

Counting the days became meaningless one midnight
when you stayed up till three to listen to my voice.

With my hand softly locked in yours
we were walking toward a beginning.

But isn't it strange?
How one phone call can turn
EVERYTHING
to NOTHING.

Half a month has passed.
We meet again unexpectedly,
walk past each other,
no hellos,
no goodbyes,
just nobodies.

Spring Elegy II

Together on a white paper
they had finished sketching and painting.
They were moving toward the final touches
when all of a sudden
he tore the whole thing apart
before the paint ever dried.

Just one apology
and I could have been all yours
But you never called again.

Spring Elegy III

I leave home in a pair of black flats
and an ivory trench coat you used to like.
My mind traces back to April
when we had EVERYTHING and NOTHING.

Afternoon small talks and midnight conversations,
I thought I had finally found my eye of heaven;
Why did you have to bring down the rain?

So here I am, drowned in silent screams
forever wondering what the reason had to be.

Spring Elegy IV

We saw through each other at first glance
and buried away each other's past romance.
I decided to take my chances,
willingly picking up after your mess.

But a handwritten note I put in your pocket
gets crumpled, forever unread,
goes straight into a trash can.
Oh, I should have known in the first place.

I will never forget how you made me feel:
small, vulnerable, and weak.
And in my head one question screams:
Was this the kind of ending you wanted?

I Left My Heart in Italy

I hop on a yellow metro at Centrale
and take a picture in front of the Duomo,
walking the rain-hugged streets without an umbrella.

We converse for an hour in each other's second language.
It is nothing personal, I am aware,
but why does my face redden at your gaze?

Your careful selection of English vocabulary
and smiles filled with mischief and concerns
won't stop echoing, I can't get them out of my head.

cont.

Did you hear my goodbye? I wanted to
look in your eyes and tell you Grazie, Ciao,
and the idea of you has been engraved since.

The next day on the plane back home
as I changed the time setting on my phone
from Rome to Seoul, I knew I had to let you go.

Stay in my past, my memories—
but please, not in my heart.

Friends

Casual, small talks are exchanged
over two cups of Princes of Wales.

As you tap, tap on the screen of your phone
browsing for a picture to show me,
I look into your ever familiar face
from the corner of my eye.

Moments like this trigger
the same question now and then;
Did you, for once, ever,
feel the same way I feel about you?

But I must hold back, mustn't I—
How could I dare pass
the parallel lines that have defined us
since you became a part of my life?

For I can never bear the fear
of going back to what we used to be:
Nobodies.

Spring Again

'Tis the season
when my right hand cannot bear to stay home.
She peeps out of the pocket
of my powder pink jacket,
eyes in thin lines,
constantly seeking for a chance to waltz with a pen.

Yikes!
Looks like she did it again:
Here's another poem.

Caffeine Overdose 524

It is a truth universally acknowledged that a single student in possession of due dates must be in want of caffeine.

So in order to keep myself awake, I decided to soak myself with caffeine. Why, how could I sleep when You are talking? Now wouldn't that be a pity and a sin. I NEEDED to stay awake.

But after three straight shots of caffeine my hands beganto ssshake and my sighgt became blurrry but i still mananged to keep myself awajke becauxe its You thats doing the talk You arethe one talking.

after two hours of paying attention to every detail that flowered out of Your lips i was exhausted i mean i could not wait to go home and just sleep for hours but when i was climbing up the staircase You called me and asked me a question i said yes and You asked me another question and i said yes and i laughed a little and You laughed too and said good bye and it was like i was taken to another dimension

And all of a sudden, all of my exhaustion went away and I could feel energy particles marathoning through my veins. Oh, isn't it funny and strange, how one small talk can turn your day around?

That is when it hit me.

Oh, I am *so* in love.

Mr. Blue

What would be the price for me
to once, call you mine?
I travel 18 miles just to see one smile,
but my sanity is torn into pieces
whenever you talk about winter, 2015.
You never laugh, always keep your chin down
and your pain, you never let any out.

Here and now, all I can offer is a small hand;
Five years from now, will things have changed?

Jayoon

Six letters, two syllables.
My name has never sounded more beautiful.

It is the way your lips part wide
and make an oo
then your tongue softly brushes against your teeth.

There is no place other than your two lips, tulips
I would forever rest my name on.

Incarnation

J, a naive-faced woman calls out
to a baby toddling around in a baby walker
as a man takes a picture of the small thing.
the baby slowly takes in the four walls
surrounding, white,
and the incarnation was complete.

J, her eyes sway from side to side
as she walks into a store on mott street.
she looks for her initial,
a letter that was engraved one winter morning.
she grabs a small pouch with the letter on it,
and the incarnation was complete.

J, she calls him from margaret's apartment.
she steps on his toes and they waltz
along to a manhattan nocturne
on and on in seoul afternoon light.
but she hears the alarm go off,
and the incarnation was complete.

Spring Again

Romance, Larghetto

I wish I did not have to travel to
the artistic city you live in.
I wish I understood every emotion
you convey in the second movement.
I wish I could hold those ivory petals
that flutter across the keys.

I wish I could.
I wish you knew.

A Great Divide

In less than 4 months, alas,
we will be 5,568 miles apart
and you will start living a time
9 hours later than mine.

I say, "Professor, I no longer care."
The Brontës, Austen, Shakespeare—
What are they to matter
when you will not be there?

Dear

if I told you how much I love you
you would run away

The Conservative Nymph's Reply to the Shepherd

He who would search for pearls
must dive below
and hold his breath for long.

Ask on to come live with you and be your love,
Bring on a thousand fragrant posies,
Recite on your words of milk and honey—
They will not change her mind.

I understand your desire a piacere
to conquer an America unexplored,
but showers of mere lip service—
They will not change her mind.

This poem was written as a response to Christopher Marlowe's poem, 'The Passionate Shepherd to His Love.'

Whatever attempt you make
to make her spread apart,
presumably like the legs of an easel—
They will not change her mind.

You shell forget about presto,
for she rather prefers largo, larghetto, adagio—
Have you not heard? It takes time and exertion
to win the brightest pearl, the crème de la crème.

He who would search for pearls
must dive below
and hold his breath for long.

A Modest Proposal

In the middle of the night
when sleep failed to visit me
I was scrolling down the screen
when a few words took me aback.

Most of them were good, surely,
written in awareness of your qualities,
but it was a few lines that concerned me,
words I'd rather you didn't look at.

But before you be disheartened
by such trivial, insolent opinions, please remember:
it was the great writers and artists, not little people,
that brought on the English Renaissance.

Thus, I hereby propose, with modesty,
that you continue your teaching with firm belief;
for there will always be a special someone out there
that deem your lessons a blessing.

Palette
(written in collaboration with Jihyun Kim)

I'm twenty-one.
Do I like it?

Too young to be an adult and too old to be a child.
Nothing is certain; future, likes, dislikes,
whom I love and whom I hate.

This March I thought I found true love
but it turned out to be no more than a sweet dream;
my mind became a blank after sunrise.
But I added that sunrise to my palette
and now it shines among my colours.

I'm twenty-one.
Yes, I got this.

This poem was inspired by IU's song, 'Palette.'

A Calling

Whether it be
the Victorian fin de siècle (engraved since 2003
when she first picked up Jane-her-air),
metaphysical poetry (it's all because of a flea),
or Shakespeare (don't you dare roll your eyes),

Let it be a sign,
Let it be a road of mine.
Let it lead me to my elected vocation,
Hand in hand with you.

Veritas

Apologies

I am sorry
it took me so long –
a whole book –
to say these three words.

I _____ you.

Thank you for being a part of my second

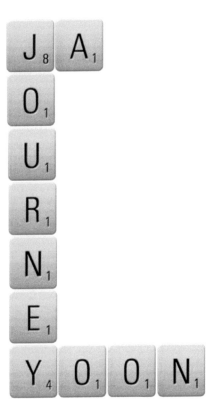